Tommy

Written by
Jason Vulpes

Illustrated by
Erika Rivera

Published by
Vulpes publishing

Printed in Australia by
IngramSpark

TOMMY WAS A YOUNG MAN,
WITH BLOND HAIR LIKE WHEAT.
JUST 20 YEARS OLD,
AND LIVING ON SMITH ST.

SMITH ST
P

AT CLUBS HE WAS SHY,
AROUND THE OTHER CUTE BOYS.
ALWAYS LEAVING ALONE,
AND RESORTING TO TOYS.

MADE A PROFILE ON GRINDER,
"LOOKING FOR DICK!"
HE NEEDED IT HARD,
HE NEEDED IT QUICK.

TOMMY 20
Hi! How are you?
I'm looking for dick!
Nice ;)

THEN LATE ONE EVENING,
HE HOOKED UP WITH BEN.
OLDER THAN THE PRETTY BOYS,
TOMMY DISCOVERS MEN.

SOME MEN WERE GENTLE,
SOME MEN WERE ROUGH.
BUT TOMMY COULD TAKE IT,
HIS ANUS WAS TOUGH.

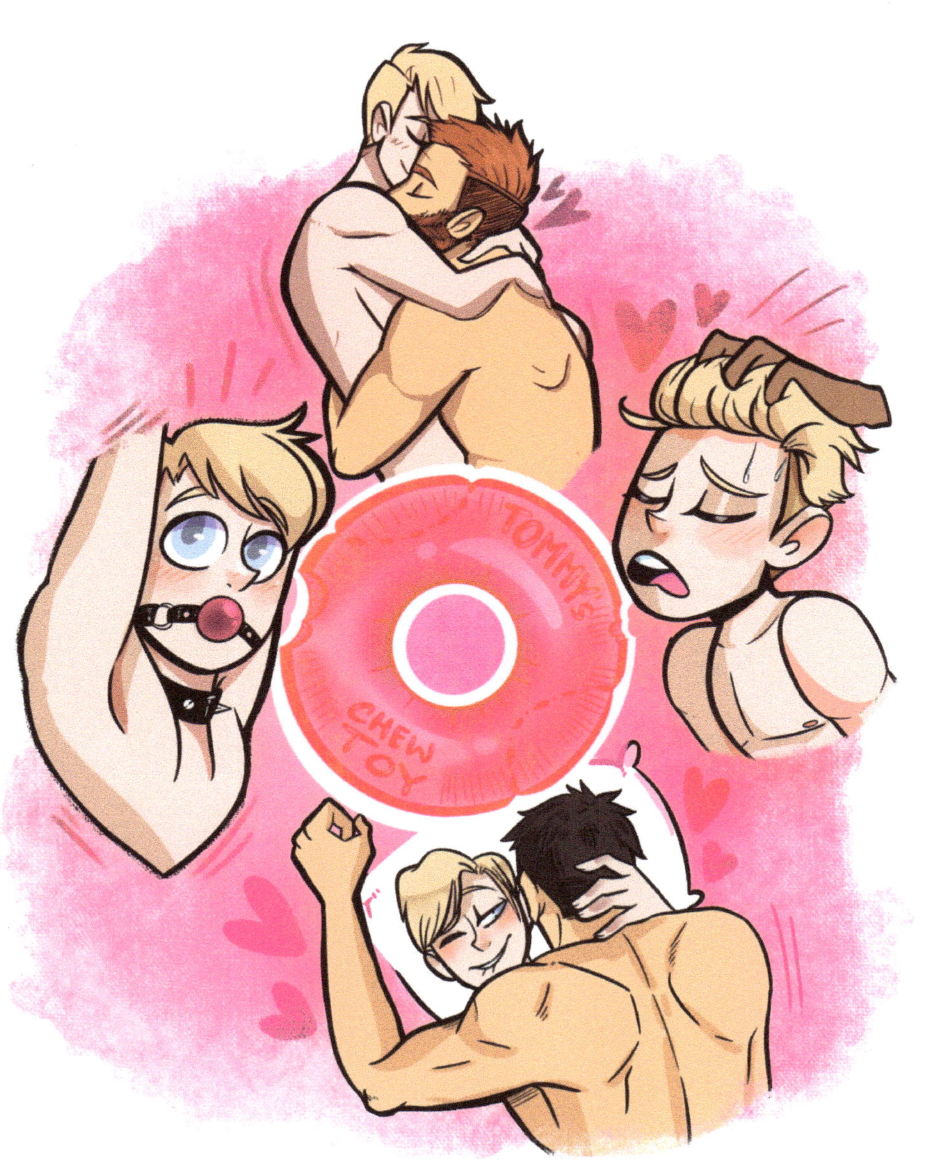
TOMMY'S
CHEW TOY

CUMMING FOR TOMMY,
WAS ALWAYS A CHORE.
THE MEN WERE ALL GREAT,
BUT TOMMY NEEDED MORE.

HE ALWAYS CAME SECOND,
HE ALWAYS CAME LAST.
UNTIL HE DISCOVERED,
THE FIVE FINGER BUTT BLAST.

HIS VERY FIRST TIME,
STUFFED LIKE A PUPPET.
HE CAME SO HARD,
COULD'VE FILLED UP A BUCKET.

HE MADE LOTS OF FRIENDS,
WHO ASKED HIM TO STAY.
HE SHOULD SPEND THE WEEKEND,
LET THEM HAVE THEIR WAY.

Boytoy

THE VERY FIRST NIGHT,
PASSED AROUND LIKE A SLUT.
HIS YOUNG HOLE WAS LOOKING,
LIKE A HOT GLAZED DONUT.

HE WAS TOLD TO BEND OVER,
IT'S BEST NOT TO STAND.
ESPECIALLY WHEN,
A FRIEND GIVES YOU A HAND.

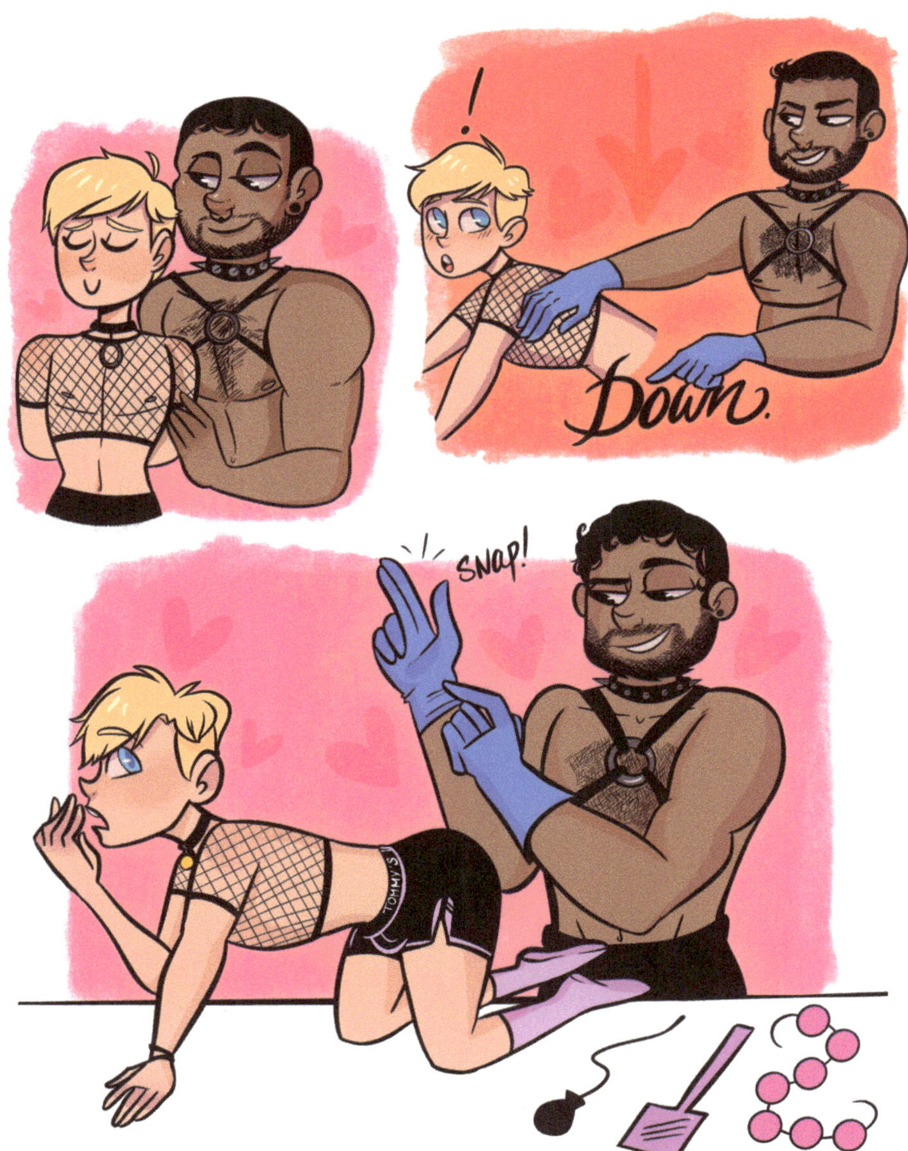
Down.
SNAP!
TOMMY'S

THEY STRETCHED HIM WIDE,
THEY STRETCHED HIM DEEP.
THEY LEFT HIM GAPING,
AND SOUND ASLEEP.

BY SUNDAY MORNING,
AFTER A WEEKEND OF LOVE.
TOMMY'S HOLE WAS LOOKING,
LIKE A SCRUNCHED UP DISH GLOVE.

DOWN AROUND SMITH ST,
YOU'LL FIND HIS CABOOSE.
READY FOR MORE,
ALL SLOPPY AND LOOSE.

SMITH ST
P